This Stargirl book belongs to:

_____

_____

_____

For the Edinburgh Book Shop,

with love and thanks

This is a work of fiction. Names, characters, places and incidents
are either the product of the author's imagination or, if real, used
fictitiously. All statements, activities, stunts, descriptions, information
and material of any other kind contained herein are included for
entertainment purposes only and should not be relied on for
accuracy or replicated as they may result in injury.

First published 2013 by Walker Books Ltd
87 Vauxhall Walk, London SE11 5HJ

2 4 6 8 10 9 7 5 3 1

Text © 2013 Vivian French
Illustrations © 2013 Jo Anne Davies

The right of Vivian French and Jo Anne Davies to be identified
as author and illustrator respectively of this work
has been asserted by them in accordance with the
Copyright, Designs and Patents Act 1988

This book has been typeset in StempelSchneidler

Printed and bound in Great Britain
by Clays Ltd, St Ives plc

British Library Cataloguing in Publication Data:
a catalogue record for this book is available from
the British Library

ISBN 978-1-4063-3341-1
www.walker.co.uk

Stargirl Academy

Madison's
Starry Spell

VIVIAN FRENCH

WALKER
BOOKS

Stargirl Academy
Where magic makes a difference!

HEAD TEACHER
Fairy Mary McBee

DEPUTY HEAD
Miss Scritch

TEACHER
Fairy Fifibelle Lee

TEAM STARLIGHT

Lily

Madison

Sophie

Ava

Emma

Olivia

TEAM TWINSTAR

Melody

Jackson

Dear Stargirl,

Welcome to *Stargirl Academy*!

My name is Fairy Mary McBee, and I'm delighted you're here. All my Stargirls are very special, and I can tell that you are wonderful too.

We'll be learning how to use magic safely and efficiently to help anyone who is in trouble, but before we go any further I have a request. The Academy MUST be kept secret. This is VERY important...

So may I ask you to join our other Stargirls in making The Promise? Read it – say it out loud if you wish – then sign your name on the bottom line.

Thank you so much ... and well done!

Fairy Mary

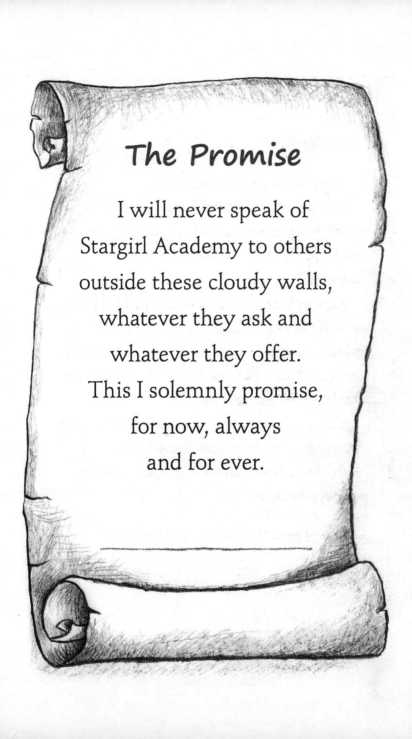

The Promise

I will never speak of
Stargirl Academy to others
outside these cloudy walls,
whatever they ask and
whatever they offer.
This I solemnly promise,
for now, always
and for ever.

The Book of Spells

by

Fairy Mary McBee

Head Teacher at

The Fairy Mary McBee

Academy for Stargirls

◆ ◆ ◆

A complete list of Spells can be obtained from the Academy.

Only the fully qualified need apply. Other applications

will be refused.

Starry Spells

Starry Spells are suitable for those
at the beginning of their career in magic,
through a little experience is helpful.

Starry Spells include such spells as:

- Solidifying
- The removal of mould
- Encouraging hens to lay

I need to swear you to secrecy. Cross your heart and hope to die – and swear not to tell anyone about us Stargirls!

Oh! I'm so silly. You don't know who I am! I'm Madison Smith. I live with my mum and my big sister. My dad (he was around back then) was so excited when she was born that he insisted she was called Arizona. Of course she hates it, and we all have to call her Izzy. Just sometimes I call her Arizona. It makes her so mad that it's funny!

But I'm not meant to be telling you about Izzy. I'm meant to be telling you about Stargirl Academy...

I bet you know all about Cinderella and her Fairy Godmother. Well, the Academy USED to be where Fairy Godmothers got trained. Then the head, Fairy Mary McBee, realised that Fairy Godmothers might be a little bit old-fashioned, so she decided to bring the whole thing up to date. She changed The Cloudy Towers Academy for Fairy Godmothers into The Fairy Mary McBee Academy for Stargirls.

Who are the Stargirls?

Girls like ME! Girls just like YOU!

We're learning about spells and magic so we can help people, just like Fairy Godmothers used to do. It's all SO amazing. We wear our very special Stargirl necklaces, and if we tap once on the pendant ... WHEEE! We can't be seen — we're completely invisible.

Isn't that just mind-blowing? I'm still in shock.

But I want to tell you what happened when the wand chose me...

Madison xxxxxxx

Chapter One

Last Monday afternoon, Izzy and I had the worst row ever. We used to get on really well, but just recently we've been fighting loads. Ever since she went to her new school, she thinks she's SO grown-up, and she can't be bothered with me. We never cuddle up on the sofa any more, and we never go shopping together. I used to love it when we did that – we used to giggle all the time, and come back with all sorts of rubbishy things that we both adored. But not now.

This particular row ended with Izzy pulling my hair and emptying my school bag all over the carpet, then storming up to her bedroom and slamming the door. My mum was FURIOUS, and said it was all my fault, but it wasn't. Well, maybe just a teeny weeny bit, if I'm honest.

This is what happened.

We were coming home on the bus – our schools are quite close, and sometimes we end up on the same one. Izzy was sitting with a tall girl, and I slid into the seat behind them. Izzy didn't say hello, or even look at me, and that made me cross.

"Hel-LO!" I said. "Little-sister alert! It's ME!"

The tall girl turned and gave me a beaming smile. She seemed much happier to see me than Izzy did. Then she looked at Izzy. "A little sister?" she said. "You never said you had a little sister."

Izzy wriggled in her seat and mumbled

 16

something like, "You never asked, Di."

Di raised her eyebrows, and turned back to me. "You look so cute. I'd LOVE a little sister like you." She heaved a massive sigh. "I'll tell you a secret, if you promise not to tell. Izzy knows, because she's my best friend. But nobody else does. Promise?"

Of course I nodded.

"I don't have any brothers or sisters. It's just me and Mum, and Mum's ill. She needs loads of looking after, and it's me that has to do it."

Di gave me a sad smile, and I saw she had tears in her eyes. Real tears! I thought Izzy would give her a hug, but she didn't. That REALLY surprised me, because Izzy's always been a total sympathy freak. She hugs little old ladies when they drop their shopping, and she hugs every shrieking baby she can get her arms round, and she cries her eyes out if anyone even mentions little lost puppies.

I wanted to ask Di what was wrong with her mum, but I was scared she'd think I was cheeky. It sounded really awful, whatever it was.

"At least I've got friends," Di went on. "Friends like your big sister Izzy. I don't know what I'd do without her." She squeezed Izzy's arm. "Izzy's going to be an angel and help me with my homework, aren't you, Iz?"

"I always do, don't I?" Izzy sounded grumpy, but Di took no notice and I thought how nice she was not to mind. Di gave Izzy's arm another squeeze. "So you'll meet me tomorrow? Before school?"

That was when I had an idea. I wanted

to make up for Izzy being unhelpful, so I said, "Couldn't she bring it round to your house?"

Di shook her head. "No good, cutie. My mum can't cope with visitors. She has to lie down all the time, and the only person she wants to see is me." She sighed again. "Poor old Mum."

"Ah," I said. I didn't know quite what to say. "I'm … I'm sorry."

Di pinched my cheek. "It's OK. I'm used to it." Then she brightened. "But I could collect it tonight. Where do you live?"

"Launceston Lane," I said. "Number 23."

I got a dazzling smile. "Thanks. Your big sister's lucky to have you. Isn't she a total poppet, Izzy-wizzy?"

Izzy nodded. She was looking cross, and I knew why. She didn't want me getting

20

friendly with someone from St Dunbow's. She never said anything about her friends there, and I was certain it was because she wanted to keep them for herself.

Di leant over and pulled Izzy's homework book out of her bag. "Let's have a look and see what we've—" The bus gave a lurch and Di dropped the book. It slid under the seat and another girl picked it up.

"This yours, Izzy?" she asked and then she looked at the book more closely. "That's odd. Why does it say A Smith?" She turned to the girl beside her. "A for Isobel? First I've heard of it!" And they both laughed.

Izzy went very pink. "It's just a mistake," she said, and she snatched the homework book back and stuffed it in her bag.

Di gave Izzy a massive nudge, and winked at me. "You need to be more careful, Iz. Doesn't she, cutie?"

"Yes," I said, and I winked back at her. She was so nice! But Izzy didn't seem to think so at all. It was weird! Di was her best friend, but Izzy was bundling her stuff together and pulling on her coat as if she couldn't wait to get away.

"Hurry up, Madison. You're so slow! It's our stop any minute—"

I looked at my sister in astonishment, and she made a stupid face at me – and that did it. I stood up and said, very loudly, "I know it's our stop, ARIZONA."

Izzy went completely purple and grabbed my arm. "You little beast," she hissed, and she hauled me down the aisle as if I was a sack of potatoes before pushing me off the bus the second the doors opened. I heard Di calling after us, something about seeing us later, but Izzy didn't answer. She stomped home without saying a word – but as soon as we were through the door she started shouting at me. She said I was interfering and I'd ruined her life and I didn't know what I'd done because I was stupid and silly and a baby – oh, all sorts of stuff. And then she shut herself in her room.

So I suppose it *was* me that started the row ... but she didn't need to pull my hair. OR throw my stuff around.

Chapter Two

After Izzy had stormed off, Mum asked what had happened. I had to confess I'd called her Arizona in front of everyone on the bus, and Mum said that was totally unfair, and it was up to Izzy to tell people if and when she wanted to. She said I'd better go and tell Iz I was sorry, but I didn't. I flung myself on my bed and pulled my diary out from under my pillow. I wanted to see how many times my big sister had been mean and horrible in the last few weeks – and it was LOADS!

"H'mph," I thought, and I wondered if it was possible to ask Fairy Mary McBee for some kind of spell to teach her a lesson.

I began to write in my diary. "If Izzy was turned into a pig for a week or two, maybe she'd be nicer when she went back to being a girl—" And THAT was when I got a Tingle in my elbow.

PING!

I felt this little electric shock and I thought, "HURRAH!" Because when the Tingle comes it means the Academy is somewhere close by, and it's time for lessons.

That probably sounds weird, so I'll explain and then it'll sound even weirder!

I think I told you the Academy used to be called Cloudy Towers, so you won't be surprised when I tell you it has lots of towers. None of us has ever seen all the rooms inside. Lily and Ava think they move around when we're not looking! (Lily and Ava are my very best friends, by the way.

And so are Olivia and Sophie and Emma.
We're all in the same team – Team Starlight.)

The Academy isn't a fixed kind of
building, though. It's on a cloud, so it can
actually float to lots of different places.

Isn't that amazing? I couldn't believe it when I was first told about it. I thought Miss Scritch was joking, until I found out that she NEVER makes jokes. She's much too serious. She's the deputy head and she's tall and thin, and she looks down her nose at us. Lily says Miss Scritch disapproves of us, but I don't know. Sometimes she can be quite nice, and although she's very strict she's always fair. And if she tells you something, you can be sure that it's true.

Now, where was I? Oh, yes. When it's time for Stargirl classes we get a Tingle, and then we have to hurry to the Academy. And that's another weird thing ... however long we spend there, we always get home at EXACTLY the moment we left, so nobody knows we've been away and they don't have to worry about us.

 28

I'd love to know how Fairy Mary McBee does it. I know it's magic, but it makes my head feel odd when I think about it. I mean, where does the extra time go? Can you fold it up and tuck it away somewhere? One day, when I'm feeling brave, I'm going to ask.

PING! The Tingle came again.

It was time to get going.

The last time I'd felt the Tingle, I'd been out in our garden, and it had suddenly filled with mist. I'd been really confused – I didn't know what was happening. I'd tried to find my way back to the house, but instead I found some steps, and the steps had led me to the Academy's front door.

This time something made me look out of my bedroom window, and sure enough it was misty again – and there was a bridge outside, even though I was two floors up!

29

I couldn't see what was at the other end, but I just KNEW what it was.

I heaved the window open and crawled out ... and a moment later I was knocking on the door of The Fairy Mary McBee Academy for Stargirls.

Chapter Three

The door was opened by Ava, and she gave me a quick hug. "Hurry up," she said. "You're late! We're all in the workroom, and Miss Scritch is muttering about not having time to learn today's spell properly."

"I came as soon as I could," I told her.

"It's OK," Ava said, and she grabbed my hand and rushed me inside. I couldn't help feeling a bit hurt, but when I stepped into the workroom Fairy Mary McBee greeted me with a beaming smile.

"Madison, dear! I'm so sorry! I was just telling Miss Scritch that your Tingle got held up. The first two times I sent it, it bounced back – were you very busy?"

"Busy?" I thought about it. I hadn't exactly been busy. I'd had Mum telling me off, of course, and I'd been really, REALLY fed up with Izzy...

"No, Fairy Mary," I said, and then something in the way she was looking at me made me explain. "My mum was cross with me. She doesn't like it when I tease my sister."

Fairy Mary McBee nodded. "I see. And you were angry too, perhaps?"

"Erm..." I hesitated, and then I couldn't help adding, "My big sister's HORRIBLE!"

Fairy Mary nodded again. "Well, well. But never mind that now. You're here, and we're delighted to see you." She snapped her fingers. "Girls! I think there's time for us all to have a hot drink while Madison sits down and catches her breath."

I made my way to the seat Ava had saved for me. Lily was on my other side, and as I slid into my chair she whispered, "Hi, Madison!" Emma, Sophie and Olivia waved. Only Melody and Jackson didn't say hello. That didn't surprise me; they always stick together. On our very first day at the Academy, they'd refused to be part of our team and had insisted on being a team of their own.

Miss Scritch gave me a chilly smile, then took a large tin tray out of a cupboard and put it on the table. She murmured something under her breath, and the very next minute the tray was full of mugs of steaming hot chocolate. There was a loud *Ooooh!* from everyone, and as Sophie and Emma handed out the mugs I looked round.

The workroom was just about the same as the last time I'd seen it. The shelves were still weighed down with tottering piles of paper. The weird-looking jars and bottles were just as dusty as before, but the spiky-leaved

34

plants hanging from the ceiling looked as if they'd grown. They were certainly much greener. The cupboards under the shelves didn't seem to be quite so full, though, and someone had changed the labels. I could see *Sharpened pencils* on one cupboard, and I was almost disappointed. It sounded much too sensible for an Academy that taught magic. Then I saw *Travelling spells, fast and slow (NB CAUTION ADVISED!!!!)* and *Helpful Answers to Unfortunate Wishes,* and I thought, "That's better!" The rusty old telescopes were still hanging on the wall, but there was a gap next to them. I was sure there'd been something there – hadn't it been something important? – but before I could ask anyone, Sophie handed me a mug, and I forgot all about the gap. The chocolate was perfect! I'd never had anything half as good.

"JEEPERS CREEPERS!" It was Lily. She was sipping her chocolate with her eyes shut in complete and utter bliss, and it made me want to hug her. She lives with an ancient old aunt, and although the aunt is LOADS better than she used to be (thanks to us Stargirls!) I don't suppose Lily has too many treats. Ava saw me looking at Lily, and she gave me a little "I know just what you're thinking" wink. I winked back. It's SO brilliant having friends like that.

Chapter Four

"Has everyone finished?" It was Miss Scritch, and we hastily drained the last of our hot chocolate and put our mugs back on the tray.

"Yes, Miss Scritch," we chorused.

"Then perhaps we can get on with what we are meant to be doing. Clear the table!" Miss Scritch waved her hand, and the mugs disappeared. That, I decided, would be a brilliant spell for when Mum wants me to wash up ... but then I began to think about it. Where did the mugs actually go? Did they get cleaned all by themselves? Or did they disappear to some special place to be washed up by elves or goblins or—

Lily dug me in the ribs, and I suddenly realized Miss Scritch had asked me something.

"Yes, Miss Scritch?" I said brightly.

She glowered at me. "I asked, Madison, if you could remember what we did in our last lesson. But perhaps your own thoughts are more interesting? If so, do please tell us what they are."

"Well … " I hesitated. "Actually, I was wondering about the mugs. They just vanished. So where did they go? And how do they get washed?"

To my amazement, Miss Scritch almost smiled. "Excellent questions. I like a practical and enquiring mind. For your information, the mugs have gone to the kitchen. They will be washed up later."

"Oh," I said. "Erm … thank you. And I do

39

remember, by the way. We learnt how to float things last time. It was a Shimmering Spell."

"Good." Miss Scritch still didn't smile properly, but she looked a lot less fierce. "Yes, indeed. So this week we are going to learn how to Solidify with a Starry Spell."

We stared at her in astonishment.

"Excuse me?" Melody often sounds grumpy, but this time she sounded as if she thought Miss Scritch was mad. "What on earth's that?"

I heard Fairy Mary McBee chuckle. She was sorting papers in a corner of the workroom, but she looked up to say, "Do show them, Miss Scritch."

Miss Scritch sniffed. "I was about to do exactly that, Fairy Mary." The tin tray was still on the table, and she pushed it across

40

until it was right in front of Melody. "Please be kind enough to pass this tray to Jackson."

"What?" Melody raised her eyebrows, and gave the tin tray a casual shove.

It didn't move.

Melody frowned, and pushed at it again. It still didn't move. "It's stuck to the table," she said. "You've put some kind of spell on it!"

Miss Scritch shook her head. "The tray is not stuck. Perhaps Jackson would like to help you lift it."

Jackson took one end of the tray, and Melody the other. Between them they managed to lift it a couple of centimetres before it crashed back down.

"It weighs a tonne," Jackson said, and she rubbed her arms. "That thing's dangerous!"

"Only in the wrong hands," Miss Scritch told her. "And it is not a question of weight. It's merely a question of solidity. Now, shall we see if any of you can achieve such a satisfactory result?"

Olivia put up her hand. "Please, Miss Scritch, what shall we use to practise on?"

Miss Scritch fished in her pocket and produced a handful of buttons. "These will do to begin with." She raised a warning

 42

finger. "One thing to remember! Never use this spell on a living creature. It won't work."

Emma giggled. "That's a shame. I'd love to Solidify my little brother. He's a pain!"

Miss Scritch was not amused. She gave Emma a frosty look, and dropped the buttons on the table.

Chapter Five

We each chose a button (mine was red) but before Miss Scritch could give us any instructions there was a flurry in the doorway, and the workroom was filled with a swirl of tiny pink stars.

"I'm so sorry I'm late!" said a breathless voice. "I do hope you haven't started without me!"

"H'm. Fairy Fifibelle Lee." Miss Scritch sounded as chilly as a snowstorm in January. "Were we expecting you?"

"Surely you didn't think I would miss seeing these utterly darling children?" Fairy Fifibelle drifted into the room, her long white hair and gauzy scarves floating gently around her. "So what are we doing today, my little dears?"

"We're on the point of learning the Solidifying Spell," Miss Scritch snapped. "How to Solidify an object. Not one of your favourites, I suspect."

Fairy Fifibelle gave a silvery laugh. "Dear Miss Scritch! How could you say such a thing?" She tweaked a curly pink feather from one of her hundreds of scarves and laid it on the table. She closed her eyes, and waved her hands. There was a flurry of bright pink stars as Fairy Fifibelle pointed to Emma. "Blow it away, dear heart."

Emma took a deep breath and blew. The feather stayed exactly where it was. Emma blew again and again … and then Olivia joined in and Sophie too. Even with all three

of them blowing as hard as they could the feather didn't move.

Jackson leant forward and picked it up.

"Wow!" she said. "It's really heavy!" She passed it to Melody. Melody gasped and passed it to Ava, who gave a little squeak and dropped it. We all heard the *thud* as it fell. I bent down to pick it up … and I could only just heave it back onto the table.

"JEEPERS!" said Lily, and that just about summed it up for all of us.

Fairy Mary McBee had put her papers down and come over to watch. "A very fine example of solidifying," she said. "I'm sure you agree, Miss Scritch!"

Miss Scritch gave an unwilling grunt of approval.

"But when would we use a spell like that?" Melody asked. "It doesn't seem much use to me."

"Oh, my darling!" Fairy Fifibelle's wings fluttered as she swooped towards Melody. "Suppose someone is on the point of taking a bite from a poisoned apple? We solidify the apple, and it drops to the ground. Lo and behold! The danger is over."

"Not if the apple drops on their foot," Melody said. "They'd be in hospital for weeks."

Fairy Fifibelle gave Melody a sharp look,

but she didn't tell her off. Instead she turned to the rest of us. "Shall we begin? And do remember, my precious ones, to point at the buttons with your little finger. The one with the star."

Oh! I'm sorry. I completely forgot to tell you about the stars on our little fingers! When we first came to the Academy, Fairy Mary McBee sprinkled fairy stars all over us, and we were each left with a tiny star on the little finger of our left hand. I love mine. When I'm in bed, and the room is very dark, I can see it glimmering ... and it reminds me that I'm training to be a Stargirl, and that makes me really happy.

Chapter Six

It turned out that Starry Spells are tricky.
There are several degrees of solidifying.
You can oversolidify, and if you do that
(Sophie did) your button is SO heavy it
falls right through the table, leaving a
button-shaped hole behind it. Miss Scritch
sighed and closed up the hole with a tap of
the wand she always keeps tucked up her
sleeve. If you undersolidify (like me) you
make the button just a little bit heavier.
Gradually, we learnt that it wasn't so much
the way we pointed our little fingers as the
way we thought about it. You had to stare
at the button very, very hard, and think
the heaviest thoughts you could ... lead,

elephants, cathedrals, towering castles...
And then the stars came floating down and
the spell worked.

After we'd all managed the buttons, Fairy
Fifibelle insisted that we tried feathers,
even though Miss Scritch said it wasn't
necessary. Actually, it was much more fun.
Feathers are so light and floaty we could
blow them up into the air before sending
them thunking down.

We practised happily until Lily missed her
feather as it drifted past her nose and sent
one of the old telescopes crashing to the
floor instead. Miss Scritch tut-tutted loudly
as she got out her wand and poor Lily went
as red as a beetroot.

"I'm truly sorry," Lily said. "Will the
telescope be OK?"

"I'm sure it will, Lily dear," Fairy Mary

51

said. "We've had far worse. Why, even our own Miss Scritch and Fairy Fifibelle Lee have had their share of accidents."

We positively gawped at Miss Scritch. It was SO difficult to think of her ever making a mistake! Somehow, it was much easier to imagine Fairy Fifibelle getting muddled.

Miss Scritch snorted. "The past is gone and best forgotten," she said. "Now, may I suggest a little revision? Do you all remember the Floating Spell? Because you'll find that extremely useful if you need to reverse Solidifying. Please watch!"

We watched with our mouths open as Miss Scritch sent our buttons whizzing round and round the room. A moment later, she sent them diving to the ground and told us to pick them up. We couldn't – they were too heavy. Miss Scritch looked extremely pleased with

herself. With a wave of her hand, she whisked
the buttons back into the air, made them loop
the loop and then dropped them neatly into
a pile on the tin tray. Fairy Fifibelle began to
clap, and we joined in.

"Now you try," Miss Scritch ordered.

Chapter Seven

We did try, but it was really difficult. I began by trying to solidify my button. It crashed to the floor just as I'd meant it to, but when I tried to float it back it zoomed straight up to the ceiling and wouldn't come down. Sophie and Ava's button whizzed out of the window and we never saw it again. Lily, Olivia and Emma tried working together, and their buttons drifted round and round their heads, but wouldn't settle back on the table.

Melody and Jackson got theirs right first time, and kept showing off; Melody even sent her button up in a shower of stars to flick mine off the ceiling. "There you are," she said.

"How did you do that?" I asked. "That's AMAZING!"

Melody gave me a sideways look. "Maybe I'm just good at magic."

I wasn't sure how to answer her, but Fairy Fifibelle swooped down to smother Melody in one of her hugs. "Darling girl! You're a star among Stargirls!"

Jackson was watching. "I don't want a hug, but I'd just like to say that I can do that too," she said. "It's easy." And she made her button knock mine off the table.

"Excellent!" Fairy Fifibelle beamed at her. "Another star of stars!" Tossing back her scarves, she pointed her finger at the button on the floor. At once it leapt back to the table, spun round and turned into a plate of chocolate biscuits. Jackson didn't say anything, but for once she gave Fairy

Fifibelle a look that was almost admiring.

Miss Scritch frowned. "These girls have already had hot chocolate," she said sharply. "Too much chocolate is NOT a healthy option!" And the chocolate biscuits turned into currant buns.

Fairy Fifibelle didn't say a word, but all of a sudden the plate was heaped with the creamiest meringues I'd ever seen. I have to admit, my mouth began to water (I adore meringues!), but then – *pouf*! – the plate and the meringues disappeared and Fairy Mary McBee was clapping her hands for silence.

"Girls! You've done very well! Very well indeed. I'm delighted with your progress. I suggest we take a short break, and then we'll get back to work." She gave both Fairy Fifibelle and Miss Scritch a faintly disapproving nod. "Thank you, ladies, but *I*

56

will provide a suitable snack. Now, my dear students, please tidy everything away, then go and wash your hands."

Chapter Eight

When we came back from washing our hands, the table was spread with a pretty red-and-white cloth, although you could hardly see it for all the food. There were sandwiches and salads and cakes and all kinds of biscuits – and I was delighted to see a large plate of meringues. There were jugs of orange juice and apple juice,

and lemonade and milk as well, and some sparkly red drink that I didn't recognize but which tasted absolutely delicious – a mix of strawberries and raspberries, but with something else too.

"It's magic," Emma said, when she tasted it. "That's what it is. Magic."

I think all of us Stargirls must have been hungry, because there wasn't much left by the time we'd finished. Fairy Fifibelle ate more than everyone else put together, but Miss Scritch just nibbled at a very plain biscuit. Fairy Mary was so busy making sure everyone had enough to eat and drink that I didn't see her eat anything, but she seemed happy. Her dear old dog, Scrabster, came out from the sitting room and helpfully ate up all the crumbs.

When at last we'd finished, Miss Scritch

came to stand behind me. "Madison! You were interested in the way we clear away our dirty dishes. Perhaps you'd like to help me with the spell?"

"OH!" I could feel myself going pink, I was so excited. "Yes, PLEASE!"

Miss Scritch pulled her wand from out of her sleeve and handed it to me. "Point this at the table, and imagine it clean and clear ... and imagine all the dirty crockery and glasses piled neatly in the kitchen."

I took the wand, hardly daring to breathe. I pointed it at the table, and did my very best to think of it the way it usually looked – well worn wood, with lots of ink stains and scratches. Then I imagined the dirty plates in a pile, and the glasses stacked up, and I sent them up into the air. Up and up they went, and behind me Miss Scritch said,

"Careful. That's good, but don't rush…"

And then I stopped. I didn't know what the Academy kitchen looked like, so I couldn't imagine it – and there was the most TERRIBLE crash as the plates and glasses hit the wall. Every single cup and plate and glass smashed into smithereens, followed by the rattle and jingle of the cutlery.

"Oh," I said, and I could feel a huge lump in my throat. "Oh, I'm so sorry. I didn't know where to send them…" I took off my glasses and rubbed at my eyes. "I'm really really, REALLY sorry!"

"As it happens, Madison, you did remarkably well." It was Fairy Mary, and she didn't sound angry at all. "We'll just do a little Reversing. We should have remembered that you've never seen the Academy kitchens. In fact, why don't YOU Reverse what happened? Then Miss Scritch can take over. Just shut your eyes, dear, and remember what everything looked like when it floated up from the table."

I shut my eyes and did my best.

Lily squealed, "Oh! OH! You've done it, Madison! All the bits have joined together and everything's hovering in mid-air! Oh,

 62

well done!" And I SO nearly opened my eyes, but I didn't, even though I could hear Miss Scritch muttering beside me. Then there was a faint rattling noise ...

... and when I did open my eyes, the table was bare. There wasn't a sign of our feast, only Scrabster hunting around for a few last crumbs.

"Phew," I said, as I handed back the wand. "Wow. Thank you very much, Miss Scritch."

Miss Scritch looked down her long nose at me, but I could tell she was just a little bit pleased. "Let us hope we have all learned from the experience," was all she said. "Fairy Mary, don't you think we should be getting ready for the Spin?"

Chapter Nine

There was a thrilled silence .. and I suddenly realized what was missing from the wall. Of course! It was the golden clock!

Well, it's not actually a clock, but I don't know what else to call it. It looks exactly like a huge gold clock, with strange signs on it as well as numbers, but it only has one hand … and it's not a hand. It's a WAND! Fairy Mary McBee's wand. Fairy Mary spins it round and round, and when it stops it points at one of us. It makes little chills run up and down my spine, I can tell you! And if it points at you, then you get to choose who you want to help, and both teams work with you in the way they think best.

We looked hopefully at Fairy Mary. She nodded, and opened the cupboard marked *Sharpened pencils*. The golden clock was inside, and she carefully lifted it out. Then she gave the wand a little shake and dozens and dozens of twinkly stars floated up into the air.

"Are you ready, dear Stargirls?" Fairy Mary asked, and her voice was suddenly different.

It was almost as if she was singing, and the whole atmosphere changed. It felt as if even the room was holding its breath as we whispered, "Yes."

"Spin, spin, spin," Fairy Mary sang. "Who will choose? Who will it be? Whose destiny will change today? Spin, wand, spin..."

The wand began to spin. Round and round it went, faster and faster until it was nothing more than a blur … and then it began to slow. Slower…

… and slower …

… and then it stopped.

And it was pointing at me.

Jackson gave a loud snort. "That's SO not fair. It never points at me or Melody!"

"The wand knows what it needs to know," Miss Scritch said firmly. "Your time will come when the day is right."

Jackson glowered. "Oh, yeah?"

"I shall ignore that remark, Jackson," Miss Scritch told her, but there was a steely glint in her eye that made me VERY glad she wasn't looking at me.

Ava pulled at my arm. "Who are we going to help, Madison? Have you got any ideas?"

"Well…" I said slowly. I was thinking hard. Who could I help?

"Remember to keep it simple," Miss Scritch warned. "Your skills are still at an early stage."

I nodded, and I'll tell you something that will make you think I should NEVER be a Stargirl. I'd actually wondered for a millisecond about asking if I could turn Izzy

67

into a pig. Isn't that dreadful? As soon as I'd thought about it, I felt terrible – REALLY terrible. But thinking about Izzy made me remember the tears in Di's eyes when she talked about her poor ill mother, and how lovely her smile had been.

And you might as well know something else. I'd liked the way Di said that I was cute. I know that might sound silly, but it was an awfully long time since Izzy had said anything like that. It would be good to help someone who actually liked me.

I made up my mind.

"Could we help my big sister's friend?" I asked. "She's called Di. She has to look after her mother, and it's very hard for her. She can't have friends round or anything. She was almost crying on the bus home from school today."

The very next minute, Fairy Fifibelle was giving me one of her hugs. "Sweet child," she cooed. "That sounds perfect. How wonderful our dear little Stargirls are, Fairy Mary!"

"They still have a great deal to learn." Miss Scritch put the golden clock away in the cupboard and shut the door with a *bang*. "Isn't that right, Fairy Mary?"

Fairy Mary McBee smiled. "Let's see how they do today," she said. "Madison dear, do you know where this friend of your sister lives?"

I shook my head. "I only know she catches the same bus as us. She gets off after we do, but I don't know how long after."

"See?" Melody sneered. "Madison doesn't even know where to start."

"Dearest Melody, that is not a problem,"

Fairy Mary said. "I'll take you to the Travelling Tower, and I'm sure you'll find exactly what you're looking for. Would you follow me, please, my darlings? Oh! Have you all got your necklaces? It's always best to be prepared."

Chapter Ten

Did I tell you about our necklaces? I might have mentioned them, but if you don't mind I'll tell you again because they're a really important part of being a Stargirl. The necklaces are very pretty, but by far the best thing about them is that they can make you invisible. Other Stargirls can see you if they screw up their eyes and look REALLY hard, but nobody else can. Not at all! Each pendant has the Academy crest on it (two crossed wands and six stars) and every time we go out on a mission and help someone, one of the stars lights up ... and it keeps on shining.

One day, I hope that I'll have all six stars

shining, and when THAT happens, guess what? Yes! I'll be a genuine, first-class, fully qualified Stargirl!

It turned out that we were all wearing our necklaces (I keep mine on almost all the time, I love it so much) and so we followed Fairy Mary McBee as she led us out of the workroom and through the sitting room.

We don't use that room much; I think it's more for our teachers – there are big squashy sofas, and there's always a lovely glowing fire. When it's cold, the flames roar up the chimney and it's wonderfully cosy. There are rows of portraits on the walls, and I LOVE looking at them because they're paintings of real Fairy Godmothers: the Fairy Godmothers who studied at Cloudy Towers years and years ago. Sometimes they smile or wave, but this time most of them were looking like ordinary pictures.

There was just one Fairy Godmother watching us today, and she gave me a tiny wink as I walked past. I winked back, and she leant forward. "Be careful, child," she said in a croaky voice. "Things aren't always what they seem, you know. Never jump to conclusions until you know all the

facts." And then, before I could answer, she sat back in her chair and looked the same as all the others.

"What did she say?" Sophie asked me.

"She told me to be careful," I said. "And she said something about things not always being what they seem."

"What do you think she meant?" Sophie looked back at the painting.

I shrugged. "I don't know. We'll have to find out!"

The Travelling Tower was at the end of a maze of long, twisting corridors, and I soon lost count of all the different turnings we took.

"I'd hate to be lost here," Olivia whispered in my ear as we filed along a long narrow passage.

I didn't agree; I'd love the chance to go exploring one day. But I didn't have time to answer Olivia because at that moment I stepped down into a small circular room … and I couldn't help gasping. All the walls were glass, so you could see in every direction.

"So here we are in the Travelling Tower! I'll leave you to have a good look round," Fairy Mary McBee told us. "And while you're here, you can make your plans for helping Madison's friend. Oh! One more thing. You don't need to worry about anyone seeing you. We're very well hidden in the clouds, and even at ground-level the tower is almost invisible … but if you want to pop out for any reason, do please remember to tap on your pendants."

Chapter Eleven

POP OUT? How could we possibly pop out? But it was too late to ask. Fairy Mary had whisked away through the door, and closed it behind her.

There was a stunned silence. Then Sophie said, "Come on. Let's have a look..."

I walked over to one of the windows, and if it had been open I would have fallen out in surprise. Truly! I don't know what I thought I'd see, but I was NOT expecting to be hovering in the air above a row of houses.

"Wow!" Olivia was beside me, and her eyes were very wide. "I don't like heights. This is scary!"

I don't mind heights, but this was different. I found myself grabbing at the safety rail in front of me as I peered down. It was extraordinary; you could actually see into the chimney pots. A couple of startled seagulls looked up, saw us and flew hurriedly away.

"Where are we? I don't recognize anything." Olivia was holding on to the rail so tightly her knuckles were white.

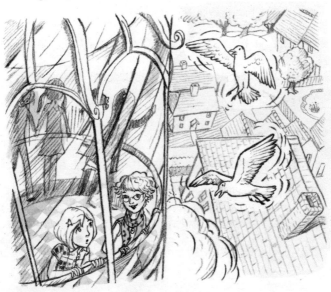

"We could be anywhere," I said, and then I realized. We weren't just anywhere. We were hovering right above my house. Those were MY chimney pots I'd been looking down!

"What a crummy house," Melody said scornfully. "Look at all the rubbish in the garden! Is this where your sister's friend lives, Madison?"

I glared at her. "No. It's where I live, actually."

"Ooops!" For once, Melody looked uncomfortable. "So why are we here?"

"I don't know," I said. "I'm sure there's a reason, though…"

"Hey, girls!" Ava was inspecting a row of buttons and levers on the back of the door. "Look! There are all kinds of instructions here. There's *Rising up* and *Sinking down*,

78

and *Elevation under difficult circumstances …* "

"But we oughtn't to touch anything," Olivia said anxiously. "It could be dangerous!"

Lily went to see what Ava was looking at. "Do you know what I think?" She sounded thrilled to bits. "I think these are the controls for the Travelling Tower!"

"I'm sure you're right," Ava said. She was looking thoughtful. "It must be some kind of lift … perhaps the Tower can detach itself from the main building. Shall we try?"

"NO! Ava! Don't touch—" Olivia shrieked, but it was too late. Ava had already pressed the button.

The Travelling Tower lurched, then lurched again. We fell over in a tumble of arms and legs, and Olivia and Sophie screamed. We were zooming downwards

and sideways, and for a moment everything outside seemed to be a whirling mass of confusion—

And then we stopped.

We were hovering ten centimetres above the ground in my next-door neighbour's front garden ... and the glass doors of the Travelling Tower had opened wide.

Chapter Twelve

For a moment nobody said anything. Then Ava said, "Ooops! Maybe I shouldn't have done that."

"I don't know." It was Jackson. "Makes things more interesting, I'd say."

Melody was looking around. "So it IS a kind of lift," she said. "That's actually quite clever."

"What if we can't get back?" Olivia sounded terrified.

Lily took her hand. "Don't worry. I'm sure Fairy Mary knows what's going on. She'd never have left us alone in the tower if she hadn't thought we'd be safe."

"And she did say the tower was invisible,

so nobody can see us as long as we stay inside," Emma pointed out.

I was thinking at a million miles per hour. Suppose the tower WASN'T invisible? What on earth would Mr and Mrs Grant say when they looked out of their front windows and saw a glass tower parked in their front garden? They'd probably have a heart attack on the spot and it would all be my fault. But when I glanced nervously across, I saw the house was in darkness. "Phew!" I thought.

I turned, and looked up at my own house. A light was on in Izzy's bedroom, but there was a thick hedge between the Grants' house and ours and I couldn't see if Mum was in the front room – but I was absolutely certain that if she'd heard anything she'd be outside in seconds.

I waited, hardly daring to breathe.

Nothing happened. Nobody appeared.

"OK, Madison." Jackson leant against the glass wall and folded her arms. "You wanted to help your sister's friend, and here we are. At the wrong house. What are your plans? Or don't you have any?"

I didn't answer her. I was still thinking. What had Fairy Mary said? *Remember to tap on your pendant if you pop out.* Was she

84

expecting us to leave the tower? She must have been. But that still didn't solve the problem. Why were we outside MY house?

And then I thought, How stupid I am! Of course the tower has brought us here. Di's going to come and collect her homework from Izzy, and all we have to do is follow her home. It was so simple and I'd missed it completely!

"It's totally OK," I said. "We're here because we're meant to be. Listen, and I'll explain." And as quickly as I could, I told them everything that had happened on the bus that morning, and my plan for following Di.

"We'll be invisible, of course," I said. "And when we get there we can help with the cooking or cleaning or something to make things better for her." In my head, I was

85

already imagining dust and dirt changed into shining floors and gleaming surfaces, while a pale invalid lying in a freshly made bed smiled happily at a triumphant Di.

"Sounds reasonable," Jackson said grudgingly. "But I think at least two of us should stay here with the tower."

"Oh, yes!" Olivia was still looking anxious. "What if it went away without us?"

Melody linked arms with Jackson. "Don't you worry, Olivia. We're Team Twinstar. We'll make sure the tower stays here while you and Team Starlight go and polish floors."

"So now all we have to do is wait for Di to arrive." I looked round at my friends. "Are there any questions?"

Emma was looking puzzled. "I do understand that Di's mum needs help, but

86

what I don't understand is why Di needs your sister to do her homework."

I stared at her. "Because Di doesn't have time – she has to look after her mum! You weren't there when she was telling me. She had real tears in her eyes. And look how she said her mum has to rest all the time—"

I stopped. I could hear quick footsteps coming along the road towards us, and as they came closer I saw Izzy look out of her bedroom window.

"Quick!" I whispered. "I'm sure that's Di coming! Tap your pendants – we mustn't be seen!"

A moment later, I heard my front door open, and Izzy's voice said, "Oh. Hello, Di."

Chapter Thirteen

We tiptoed out of the Grants' garden and peered round into my garden. It was beginning to get dark, but we could see Izzy standing on the doorstep. I wasn't totally surprised to see that she was frowning. I had no idea what was going on with my big sister, but she didn't seem to like anyone any more. She certainly didn't look at all pleased to see her friend. I couldn't see Di's face, but I was sure she was smiling her huge wide smile.

"Aren't you going to ask me in?" Di asked.

Izzy shook her head. "Here's your history homework," she said, and handed Di a couple of pieces of paper.

Di gave it a quick look. "You haven't written much."

"That's all I had time to do," Izzy told her.

"OK." Di nodded. "And weren't we meant to write a poem for English as well?"

"I don't think so," Izzy said. "I'll check." She disappeared back into the house, closing the door behind her. Di leant against the wall outside, humming cheerfully.

When Izzy came back, she was holding her school bag. She pulled out her homework notebook, but before she could open it Di stretched across and took it.

"I'll keep hold of this," she said, and then she turned and walked quickly away. "Bye, Izzy!" she called as she went through the gate, right in front of us. "See you tomorrow!"

My sister stayed on the doorstep for a moment, looking after her. I couldn't see her face properly in the gloom, but she looked weird. Sort of droopy. I almost ran forward to ask her if she was all right, but she suddenly stood up straight, turned round and went back inside, slamming the door behind her. I hesitated, but Ava took my hand.

"Come on! We need to get going! Di's walking very fast!"

Sophie, Olivia and Lily were already heading up the road. Ava, Emma and I hurried after them.

I didn't say anything, but I was feeling extremely odd. I kept telling myself that it was all fine, and Di had taken the notebook because she needed to borrow it for some reason, but it didn't make sense. And then Emma said, "Please don't mind my saying this, Madison, but I think something nasty was going on there – and you can tell me I'm wrong because you know that girl much better than I do – but I have to tell you what I think."

92

We were almost running, Di was going so fast, and it felt as if my mind was running too. Was Emma right? I think I knew even then that she was, but I didn't say anything.

On and on we went. We turned the corner at the end of the road, and Di was still walking. All the way down Bellsfield Street she marched, right to the very far end. A couple of times she looked over her shoulder as if she'd heard something, and I caught my breath – were we making too much noise? But she didn't stop until she was outside a tall house at the end of a terrace. It had marble steps leading down to the pavement, and a massive front door with frosted glass panels. It looked very grand.

Di fished in her pocket for a key, opened the front door, and went inside. The door shut behind her, and we heard the lock click loudly.

We stood and stared at each other.

What did we do now?

Chapter Fourteen

Sometimes I'm SO stupid. I'd never ever thought about how we'd get inside Di's house. When I'd decided to help her mum, I'd imagined the front door left wide open, or a friendly kind of back door that was never locked. But this house was like a fortress. It had spiky railings all round, and although there was a back gate it was locked with a huge padlock. A notice was pinned on the gate. It said, "PLEECE BEEWAR OF THE DOG!" And there was a picture of something that looked like a snowball.

"Oh, no!" Sophie said. "A dog! That's all we need."

Emma peered at the notice. "A little kid

wrote this," she said, "so maybe it's only a toy dog."

Sophie didn't look convinced. "Maybe we should go back to the Travelling Tower. If we went up into the air, we might be able to see over the walls."

"But it's getting dark," Ava told her. "We wouldn't be able to see a thing."

"What about peering through the letter box?" Lily suggested.

"Or," I said slowly, "we could knock on the door. Then when Di comes to answer it, I could slip inside…"

"I'll come with you," Ava said at once. "You can't go on your own."

"Me too," said Lily, and Emma nodded.

Olivia and Sophie hesitated.

"But what if we all get locked inside?" Olivia asked.

96

"It might be best if you stay out here," I said. "You and Sophie. If we don't come back, you can run and fetch Melody and Jackson."

"We'd be fetching Fairy Mary," Sophie said firmly, and then she paused. "Um. Er. Madison…"

"I know," I said. "You didn't think Di was as wonderful as I made her out to be."

Sophie nodded. "Sorry."

I swallowed. "No. I … I think you might be right. I'm sorry."

"Don't be!" Sophie shook her head at me. "It's only because you always think the best about everyone. That's why we like you! Go on. Go and knock, and maybe you'll prove us all wrong."

"OK," I said, and I jumped up the steps, Ava, Lily and Emma close beside me. There

97

was a massive iron knocker, and I gave it a good loud BANG!

Then we stepped back, and waited.

At first I thought nobody was going to answer, but at last we heard footsteps. A moment later the door swung open, and a woman stood in the doorway. She was small and pretty with bright pink cheeks, and as she looked around a couple of little boys came running out to join her.

"Who is it, Mum? Who's here?"

"I don't know," their mum said. "I can't see anyone."

"Maybe it's a fairy!" one little boy said.

"Or an ogre!" said the other, and they collapsed in giggles.

Their mother smiled at them. "Whoever it was, they're not here now."

And then Di appeared. "Who was that, Mum?" she asked. "Nobody ever knocks

on our door. We should never have come to this stupid place."

I'm amazed Di and her mother and her brothers didn't hear us gasp.

MUM? That was Di's mum?

"I hate it here," Di went on. "I have to go to a stupid school, and I don't know anyone. Why can't we go back to Bleffield?"

Her mum sighed. "We've been through this a thousand times, Di. You know we can't. Dad's job is here now, and the boys are happy at their school. You'll just have to try a bit harder—"

"WOOF! Woof woof woof WOOF!"

The dog was big, and bouncy, and very, very hairy. It came running through the hallway, and it saw us. I know it did.

"WOOF!" it said, and it leapt towards us, tail wagging madly.

And we ran ... but not before I'd seen Izzy's homework notebook lying on a table in the hallway.

Chapter Fifteen

Have you ever been chased by a dog? A big friendly dog who wants to play when you don't want to?

We couldn't shout at him, because we'd have been heard. I tried whispering, "Sit!" But he didn't take the slightest notice. The trouble was, he was so big. If he'd jumped up at us, we'd have been knocked right over.

We ran and we ran, and he bounced round us, barking as if it was the best game he'd ever played. And then we realized Di and her brothers were running after him ... and that meant they were running after us, even though they didn't know it.

We could hear them shouting, "Wallis!

 102

WALLIS! Come back! Come back this minute!"

Anyone watching would have thought it was hilarious. But we didn't. We thought it was dreadful! We puffed and panted and Olivia got a terrible stitch and we had to half carry, half drag her – until finally we staggered up to the Travelling Tower and flung ourselves inside … and Wallis bounded in too.

"WOOF!" he barked as he began to lick Olivia's knees. "Woof woof WOOF!"

"I don't like this," Olivia wailed. "Take us back to the Academy!"

"Push that dog OUT," Melody hissed. She was madly pressing buttons and pulling at levers. "I can't get the Tower to lift up with him inside!"

I slipped out of the Tower and into the Grants' garden, so I could look back along the road. Luckily Di had been slowed down

104

by her brothers because they couldn't run as fast as she could, but they were getting closer at an alarming rate. They couldn't see Wallis yet, but I was sure they could hear him because he wouldn't stop barking.

"Madison! You've got to do something!" Jackson was standing at the door of the Travelling Tower.

She was right. Di was only a stone's throw away. I grabbed Wallis's collar and heaved him into the garden and then through the gate and out onto the pavement. He came happily, but when I tried to leave him there he wouldn't stay. I had to stand holding him while Di and her brothers came sprinting towards me. And then, just as I thought I could safely let go, Wallis twisted round and jumped up at me. I staggered, arms flailing, and I managed to stay on my feet – but my necklace fell off at exactly the moment when Di and her brothers came rushing up.

"Cutie!" It was Di. "Where did you spring from? You've caught him! Well done! You're a star!"

"He's a very bad dog," one of her little brothers said. "He never does what we tell him! We have to keep the back door locked so he doesn't escape."

"He's a nice dog," I said feebly. I was so shocked by what had happened that I couldn't even think. Was I still with Team Starlight? Or could I have fallen back into my real life?

I glanced down at the pavement and there was no sign of my necklace. It had vanished.

I felt sick. Would I ever get back to the Academy? But before I could worry any more, someone grabbed me and hugged me and dusted me down and kissed me – and Izzy was shouting at the top of her voice.

"What have you done to my little sister? Were you bullying her too? If you were, I'll … I'll KILL you!"

Di gasped. Her arms flailed wildly in the air, and I thought she was trying to hit Izzy … but she wasn't. She was trying to run away … but she couldn't. She swayed from side to side, but her feet were stuck to the ground.

She couldn't move.

From high up above I thought I heard a tiny cheer … or had I imagined it?

Chapter Sixteen

There was a huge silence before one of Di's brothers said in a very small voice, "Our Di isn't a bully. She's nice."

"She's *not*!" I'd never heard Izzy sound so fierce before. "Ever since I started at St Dunbow's, she's been HORRIBLE! She makes me do her homework and she copies from me during lessons! And I have to do what she says, or—" Izzy stopped, and went pink— "she'll tell everyone I'm called Arizona and they'll all laugh at me. It's so unfair! When we first met, I *really* liked her, and we swapped secrets. I told her how I hated being called Arizona, and she told me about her mum…"

Izzy's voice died away. She looked down at the little boys. "Is Di your SISTER?"

Wide-eyed, they nodded.

"So do you look after your mum too?"

The boys stared. "Mum looks after us," said one.

"And she looks after Di," said the other.

"And Dad," the first one added.

"WHAT?" Izzy swung round and glared at Di.

Even in the yellow glow of the street lights, I could see that Di was deathly pale. She hung her head. "Sorry," she muttered.

"But why?" Izzy took hold of Di's jacket and shook her. "Why did you say that about your mum?"

"I hate St Dunbow's. Nobody ever talked to me," Di mumbled. "You were nice, and I wanted you to be my friend."

110

"Funny way to go about it," Izzy said, but she let go of Di's jacket.

Di nodded. She looked completely miserable. "I was really mean. I won't do it again. Promise."

"And what about my homework notebook?" Izzy demanded. "I'll be in trouble if I don't have that tomorrow."

"I know." Di was so embarrassed she was whispering. "That's why I took it." She was staring at the ground and twisting her hands round and round. "I didn't want to be horrible to you – really and truly I didn't – but once I'd started, I couldn't stop. And you never said anything. You went on being nice, and that made me worse than ever…"

She stopped, and I could see that she was trying her very hardest not to cry.

Now this is where things get weird.

112

Seriously weird.

Do you know what?

I felt sorry for Di. I really did. It's horrid being in a new place with no friends. I enjoy being part of Team Starlight so much that it makes me want to be friends with everyone else.

Is that mad?

Probably.

So, even though I wasn't wearing my necklace and I wasn't at the Academy, I decided to try something. I shut my eyes and I imagined Izzy's notebook lying on that table in Di's hall. I thought of Floating – of clouds and hot-air balloons, seagulls and kites – and I imagined the notebook coming nearer and nearer and nearer … and then I Solidified it.

SPLAT!

I heard it hit the pavement and I opened my eyes.

"Oh, look," I said quickly as I picked it up. "Here you are, Iz! Were you bringing it back to her, Di?"

Di was staring at me as if I was the world's greatest magician. Well, I suppose I was, just at that moment. In a way.

"How…" Di began. But she didn't go on. She handed the notebook to Izzy. "I really am sorry," she said, and she sounded as if she meant it from the bottom of her heart. "I won't bother you any more. I'll do my own homework. And I'll sit by myself. I won't bother you again … promise."

She turned, and took hold of Wallis's collar. "Come on, twins. Let's go home." Her voice broke, and I saw tears on her cheeks.

114

And then my soppy big sister gave her the most ENORMOUS hug, and said she'd be looking out for her in the morning.

Chapter Seventeen

Izzy and I stood and watched Di and her brothers walking away down the road for a moment before we went back to our house.

"Do you think she means it?" I asked.

Izzy smiled. "Oh, yes," she said. "I'm sure she does." And she picked me up and whirled me round. "Thanks, Maddy!"

"What for?" I couldn't think of anything I'd done – apart from the notebook, of course, but she didn't even know about that.

"Everything! If it hadn't been for you, I'd never have stood up to her – never! But when I looked out of my window and saw you and her and that enormous dog, I thought she'd come back and was being

 116

horrid to you. Hey! When I've finished my homework, come and cuddle up on the sofa, and we'll plan the best shopping trip ever and we'll go next weekend!"

"YES!" I said, and Iz blew me a kiss and went running up the stairs. A moment later, she was back.

"I just wanted to say," she said, "you can call me Arizona any time."

"Oh." I suddenly felt uncomfortable. "I'm … I'm really sorry I did that."

Izzy laughed. "Don't be. It was the best thing ever! Guess what? I'm going to write it all over my homework notebook and anyone who teases me had better watch out!" And she zoomed off again.

I waited a moment to make sure she was gone, and then I ran outside.

"Please let them still be there!" I whispered. "Please please PLEASE!"

There were still no lights in the windows next door. I hurried into the garden.

"Lily!" I whispered. "Emma? Ava? Can anyone hear me?"

There was no answer.

I ran to and fro across the grass, trying to find some trace of the Travelling Tower – but it was gone.

118

My stomach felt full of ice, and I shivered.

I'd blown it. I was a failure. I'd got it all completely and utterly wrong … and I'd never see my friends at the Academy again. It was only our second mission, and I'd managed to be a failure.

Chapter Eighteen

I wiped my nose on my sleeve, and made my way up to my room. I couldn't even be bothered to turn on the light; I wanted to crawl under my duvet and feel sorry for myself and, if I'm being truthful, cry my eyes out.

There was something shining on my bed. Two tiny sparkles of light, so bright I blinked. I hurried to look, and there – neatly laid on my pillow – was my necklace. But it was different! The last time I'd worn it, only one of the stars had been twinkling, but now there were two. TWO STARS!

"YES!" I yelled, and I didn't care who heard me.

"Madison?" Someone had answered.

I ran to the window, and flung it open. The bridge was gone, but the Travelling Tower was shimmering right outside.

"You took your time," Sophie said. "We've been waiting for ages! We thought we were going to have to go without saying goodbye."

"Goodbye?" I asked.

Olivia nodded. "Fairy Mary said we could have an extra five minutes to say goodbye to you, but then we've got to go home."

"We saw everything that happened." Ava was leaning precariously out of one of the windows. "Did you like our Solidifying Spell?"

I looked blank. "What spell?"

121

Ava giggled. "It was Melody's idea. When your necklace fell off, we thought we'd better take the Tower away in case someone found us, and also we could see better from higher up. We saw Di trying to run away from your sister and Melody said we should make her stand still and take what was coming to her."

"But you can't Solidify people," I said. "Miss Scritch said so."

Jackson looked superior. "It takes brains to work magic properly, Madison. You can't Solidify people, you see, but you CAN Solidify shoes."

"It took all of us together to get it right," Emma said. "But we did it!"

"THANK YOU," I said, and I really, really meant it.

The Travelling Tower gave a twist and a lurch, and I could see Olivia doing her best

122

not to scream. Instead she said, "We've got to go – but we'll see you very soon!"

"And Fairy Mary says to say WELL DONE!" Lily added.

And then, blowing kisses as they went, the Tower took them up and up and up in the air until I couldn't see anything but the stars twinkling in the night sky …

… but I went on waving, just in case.

Madison's Word Search

Can you find all these words in my word search?

Lily	Spin
Madison	Starlight
Sophie	Magic
Ava	Solidifying
Emma	Necklace
Olivia	Golden Wand
Melody	Star
Jackson	Good deed

```
                    Z  Y
                    Y  K
                 Y  L  I  L
                 E  D  V  Z
              L  C  A  L  F  N
              O  A  U  E  R  U
  Q X W K J I N H L I V M D E E D D O O G
  P S T Q D M O W K U A H I S D U I F M S
    J T J Q E S D C V B T O N V M A W P
    Y A Y L I N E Y T L A M A I K I
    R R O D D N V I W B A V X N
       Z D A W T D N T J I V T
    E U Y M H I E M N L A S A S
    M N L G F D J I O L C C K G
  K M K I Y L N M H H O B O K A X
  X A L I O E V      X P C O M S V
W W R N G U L        R O V E A O W
P A G J V            S X K G N
V T W J              Y P I K
O                          M C
```

Madison Smith

Loves: Shopping with her sister

Favourite colour: Purple

Can't help: Being curious

Starsign: Aries

Favourite food: Meringues

Good at: Thinking the best of people

One Token
www.stargirlacademy.com

One Token
www.stargirlacademy.com

One Token
www.stargirlacademy.com

Collect your FREE Stargirl Academy gifts!

In each Stargirl Academy book you will find three special star tokens that you can exchange for free gifts. Send your tokens in to us today and get your first special gift, or read more Stargirl Academy books, collect more tokens and save up for something different!

3 Tokens — Bookmark

7 Tokens — Star rubber

15 Tokens — Set of star transfers

5 Tokens — Sparkly pencil

13 Tokens — Door hanger

Send your star tokens along with your name and address and the signature of a parent or guardian to:
Stargirl Academy Free Gift, Marketing Department,
Walker Books, 87 Vauxhall Walk, London, SE11 5HJ

Closing date: 31 December 2013

Stargirl Academy

A message from Sophie

Hi! This is me, Sophie – and I'm hoping SO MUCH that you're going to want to read my story!

I don't have a big sister like Madison, but I DO have a little brother, Pete. He's OK – just as long as he has somewhere to rush around and play aeroplanes. When he hasn't, he's trouble. BIG trouble. It took a lot of magic, and a surprise for Jackson, to sort it out!

Love, Sophie xx